For Sue with best wishes.

M. N.

Text copyright © 1998 Margaret Nash
Illustrations copyright © 1998 Jim Eldridge

The right of Margaret Nash to be identified as the
author of this Work and the right of Jim Eldridge to
be identified as the illustrator of this Work has been
asserted to them in accordance with the Copyright,
Designs and Patents Act 1988.

This edition first published in Great Britain in 1998
by Macdonald Young Books, an imprint of
Wayland Publishers Limited

Typeset in 16/24pt Garamond Book

Printed and bound in Belgium by Proost N.V.

Macdonald Young Books
61 Western Road
Hove
East Sussex BN3 1JD

Find Macdonald Young Books on the Internet
http://www.myb.co.uk

ISBN 0 7500 2384 8

MISSION UNDERGROUND

The Making of Mr Brunel's Splendid Tunnel

Margaret Nash

Illustrated by Jim Eldridge

MACDONALD YOUNG BOOKS

Isambard Kingdom Brunel 1806–1859

Isambard Kingdom Brunel was one of the world's greatest railway engineers. The son of Marc Brunel, who built a tunnel under the River Thames, Isambard built bridges, railways, tunnels and steamships. Below are just a few of his achievements.

1830   He wins a competition for his design of the Clifton Suspension Bridge over the River Avon. The bridge is begun a year later but is completed after his death.

1833   Made chief engineer of the Great Western Railway.

1836   Work begins on Brunel's Box Tunnel in Wiltshire. (The GWR need the tunnel for the line to run between Chippenham and Bath, so that the complete line can run from London to Bristol.)

1837   His Great Western steamship is launched and takes people from Bristol to America in 1838.

1838   The first section of the Great Western Railway is opened, and the Maidenhead Bridge is completed.

1841   The Box Tunnel is completed, enabling the whole GWR line from London to Bristol to be used in 1841.

1843   Brunel's *Great Britain* steamship is launched.

1854   Paddington Station in London is opened.

1855   Brunel designs a hospital for the Crimea.

1858   His *Great Eastern* steamship is launched.

1
THE STRANGER

Isaac sprang up and let his paper fall to the ground as a large hare leapt across the field opposite. He ran alongside the hedge to watch. When he got back a man on a horse was looking down at his drawing.

"That's a good sketch, boy. Is it that group of trees over there?"

"Yes, Sir, only I can't get them right." The man climbed down from his horse, and took a pad from under his arm. Isaac watched as he sharpened a pencil on sandpaper and began to draw.

"I never go anywhere without my sketch book," the man said, squatting down beside Isaac. He peered at the trees. "If you think of the trees as triangles like this – it helps." He drew three triangles and put squiggles into them, and before you could say 'tree' there were three leafy trees on the paper.

"There you are. I used to draw the trees near the River Avon. That's when I first thought of building a suspension bridge over it."

A dull thud in the distance made them both look up. Isaac knew what it was. Every time the gunpowder went off in the tunnel being dug under Box Hill, he worried. His father was working as a ganger there for Mr Brunel, the chief engineer of the Great Western Railway. Isaac remembered a ganger called George Bailey who'd been crushed under a fall of bricks.

"There goes another blast," said the man. He tore the sketch out of his book. "Here you are, boy. You keep at your drawing. You never know where it might lead you!" The stranger mounted his horse, and rode off.

Isaac slipped the drawing inside his sketch-pad. He *would* keep on drawing, even though his father called it 'girl's stuff'. He suddenly remembered his father would be home tonight as it was Saturday. Isaac wished he could come home every night but he knew that was impossible.

As a ganger, his father was in charge of the navvies building the Box Tunnel. Through the week he stayed there in huts with his men. He worked at least twelve hours a day, and it was not unknown for him to work two twelve-hour shifts without sleep.

The smell of fresh bread wafted towards Isaac as he opened the cottage door. Gran had bacon boiling in the pot and a thick yellow cheese on the table.

"Best eat now, love," she said.

"Oh, Gran can't we wait?" She shook her head. "You know how late your father can be when he's been out with his men." Isaac sighed.

He could hear his father's words now.

"It's thirsty work down below, and if I want the best out of my lads I must share a jar of ale with 'em on pay day. You know that, my son." Isaac sighed again. He knew all right.

2
THE DARE

The next day there was Church in the
morning, with Father and him in their best
clothes, and Gran in her Sunday bonnet. After
Church his father seemed in a good mood.

"Do you think we could go to Bristol docks
and see Mr Brunel's iron steamship, the
Great Britain being built?" Isaac asked him.

"Some day Isaac."

"I mean now, today, Father? We could walk
up Brandon Hill and see it. It's been there for
over two years."

"No Isaac. Sometime when the day is special we'll go. We'll visit his suspension bridge at Clifton too. See how far they've got building that. But not today."

"Oh, let's go soon, Father. This ship will be the *largest* ship in the world." But his father was already yawning and sinking into his chair.

"Leave me be, boy." Isaac knew his father
would sleep all afternoon. He doubted there
would ever be a day special
enough for the trip.

"He'll take you one day,"
said his grandmother, taking
a cake out of the oven.

"That Mr Brunel must be some fellow to
design steamships as well as railways and
bridges. They say he works on his sums
all night. He designed his own carriage,
Isaac, so he can travel and sleep in it. A long
black thing it is. The railway workers call it
'The Flying Hearse'."

Isaac nodded, "Father says Mr Brunel is the best engineer there is; he gets on well with everyone, and isn't afraid to get his hands dirty down in the tunnel."

"I believe his father, Marc Brunel, is building a tunnel too. His is under the River Thames. I heard our Mr Brunel had a terrible accident in his father's tunnel, after saving a man's life. Clever men, those two. Now run over to the Kembles with that cake. Mrs K. must be beside herself, with her husband not working and all those mouths to feed."

Isaac took the cake. Mr Kemble, or Bullhead as he was nick-named, had been in a fight with some of the other navvies and was still recovering.

Isaac delivered the cake then sat down at the end of the lane to draw.

"Hey that's really good, Isaac." He looked up to see little Betsy Kemble with a big wooden pram, and a small child clawing her skirt.

"Can I see what else you've drawn? Oh what's this?"

She was looking at the stranger's trees.

"A man on horseback drew those," said Isaac.

"What did he look like?" she asked.

"Small, dark, bushy eyebrows, posh tailcoat and all that. Said he always carried a sketch-book with him."

By now Betsy's brother, Harry, had joined them. "Did he ride off towards the tunnel?" he asked.

"Yes. Why?"

"I bet I know who that was."

"Who?"

"It sounds like Mr Brunel. You know the chief engineer of the whole Great Western Railway, the tunnels, the lines – everything. People said it was impossible to build a tunnel under Box Hill but he's *doing* it! And he's up here this week. Folks say he's got plans for a railway station in the village too."

"Crikey! How do you
know these things Harry Kemble?"

Harry grinned. "Well I'm not stuck in a
schoolroom like you, Isaac. I hear things.
Fancy him talking to you, eh!" The little child
started whimpering. Betsy handed back
Isaac's paper, and lifted her onto the pram.
She began rocking it.

"Could you draw my picture sometime, Isaac?" she said. "Could I be in a crinoline and as pretty as a princess?" Isaac looked at her ragged dress.

"If you like, Betsy. But I think crinolines look stupid don't you, Harry?"

"Like tea cosies," said Harry, "big and barmy!" They watched Betsy push the pram down the lane. Isaac slung a stone at the hedge.

"I'm not going to school tomorrow either. I'm going to find this Mr Brunel. See if it was him," Isaac said.

"What if he's down the tunnel?" said Harry. "I bet you daren't go down there."

"I bet I dare," said Isaac.

"Not a tame goose like you. You wouldn't."

"I dare, so there."

"Well, fetch me a candle out, then I'll believe you."

"All right bufflehead," said Isaac, "I'll go down tomorrow and get you one."

3
TROUBLE AT THE TUNNEL

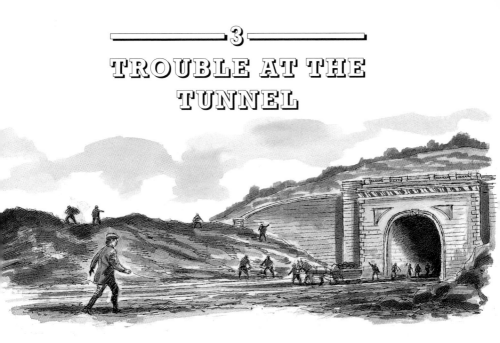

Early next morning, Isaac fed the family pig, then rushed over the fields to the tunnel.

High on top of its splendid gateway the stonemasons had chipped in the final decorations. Behind them, reaching back as far as he could see, were horses either pulling wagons or winding the ropes from the tunnel shafts. Isaac supposed he should be brave and go down one of those shafts in the tubs, but they were scary. He carried on towards the huge opening in the hillside.

"Mind out, boy." Isaac stumbled as a
wagon full of bricks ground past. He rubbed
the dust from his eyes and pulled the
woollen scarf over his mouth. Maybe he
would just go down inside the tunnel, get a
candle for Harry Kemble, and come out
without looking for Mr Brunel.

Carts, with stones spilling from them, passed near him. Isaac pressed against the tunnel entrance to let a line of workmen by and caught a glancing blow from one of the pickaxes. Stopping to rub his shoulder, he heard someone moaning and saw a man sitting at the back of the water butt. The man leaned sideways and grabbed Isaac's ankle.

"A drink, boy! Get me a drink." Isaac could see the man's leg, though bandaged, was still bleeding. His face was covered in sweat.

"Sir, let go and I'll get you some water?" Suddenly the man slumped sideways. Quickly, Isaac scooped water from the butt and splashed it onto the man's face. He came to and started moaning.

"Hurt his leg when he fell in the tunnel," said a nearby worker. "Where are you from boy?"

"From the... the village, Sir."

"I should get back there at once. It's far too dangerous for you here. You can take him with you, for there's none of us can spare the time." Isaac stared in amazement as the big man heaved the injured navvy onto a wheelbarrow, and spread the injured leg along a plank. "Steam Mill Cottages, then right down the lane. He'll tell you where."

"Yes, Sir." There seemed nothing he could do but obey. Isaac took the wheelbarrow and pushed it back to the village, his arms aching with trying to avoid the bumps. He was glad when two farm workers stopped them.

"Look, that's our Sam!" shouted one of them.

"He got hurt in the tunnel," explained Isaac.

"Oh, not again," they said.

The bigger of the two took the handles of the barrow. "What have you been doing this time our Sam?" He turned to Isaac. "Thanks kindly, lad."

He touched his cap and with that they were off. Isaac watched them go.

It wasn't even the end of school time. He sat down behind a hedge and stretched out his legs in a patch of sunlight.

"Got the candle then did you, Isaac?" It was Harry Kemble.

"Oh hello, Harry." He started to explain about the man's injured leg. Harry sat down beside him and listened.

"Ah well, it happens." He stood up. "You stick to drawing, Isaac. You never were one for danger. Me, I'll probably end up digging a tunnel too one day."

They walked to the end of the lane and parted company. But seeing that man had awakened something in Isaac. Men risked their lives every day in that tunnel. He could at least go there once and get the candle. He needed to do that for himself, as well as for Harry.

TERROR DOWN BELOW

Isaac went to his school as usual the next day, and the next, but his mind was not on his work. He was determined to go back to the tunnel for that candle.

"I'll get your candle when it stops raining," he told Harry Kemble.

"Ah go on," said Harry. "I bet you never do."

"I keep my promises," said Isaac. "You'll have your candle, and in its candle holder."

As soon as the ground had dried up a little, Isaac knew he had to go and get the candle. This time he set off for the other end of the tunnel two kilometres away.

Over the hill he went, by the Tunnel Inn and the smoking lime kilns, past the blacksmiths, until at last he was running down the other side. What if he got stopped and sent on an errand? What if his father saw him? Isaac slowed down and made a decision. He wouldn't creep in through the portal like a frightened animal. He would go down one of the tunnel shafts like a man.

He drew himself up to his full height,
pulled his cap down over his forehead then,
before he could change his mind, called to
the boy working the horse-drawn gin.

"Let me down please, will you?"

The boy nodded. Isaac climbed into the muddy iron tub. He daren't look down. The sight of the horse beginning to walk round the drum was bad enough. The tub rocked. The daylight disappeared. His stomach was heaving like the sea. Down he went, down, down towards the smell of gunpowder.

His heart was surely beating its way out of his body. All this for a candle. Why oh why hadn't he just got one from the candle factory down the road. BUMP!

He was at the bottom. He climbed out, and began making his way along the uneven tunnel floor. There was no going back now!

Cold water dripped down his neck, making him cringe and the dust started him coughing till his throat hurt. Through the haze of flickering candles came the sounds of hammers and picks smiting the rocks. He looked for a candle but they were all above him, out of reach. Then suddenly the pathway was going up the side of the tunnel to a rockface, to where men were

hammering. He stopped in a pool of light. This candle here would do. He tugged at the candle holder. It remained firmly in the wall. Steadying himself against a wooden stay, he pulled as hard as he could and the candle holder with its long spike came out of the wall. At the same time a noise like a bugle being blown sounded through the tunnel.

"Mind yourself," warned two men running towards him. Everyone had stopped hammering. There was an eerie silence. Isaac stood still. Then a thunderous noise ripped through the tunnel. The world was ending! The noise wouldn't stop! Isaac dropped his candle and crouched in the darkness.

Isaac opened his eyes. He stood up.

"All right there?" said a voice.

"Yes, thanks."

He wafted the dust away from his face.
An even stronger smell of gunpowder lay
across the tunnel. What a blasting that had
been, and now there was cheering echoing
along the walls.

"Over there," someone yelled. The men
rushed on. Isaac followed. No way was he
going to be left behind. "Light the candles!"

Through the greyness, blobs of hazy
yellow appeared. Suddenly Isaac felt at
ease with the tunnel, used to it, part of the
crowd there. It was getting lighter.
Everyone was yelling and he could
sense an air of excitement.

"They're through.
They're through."

"No!"

"Yes, through
to the end."

Now Isaac could see a hole ahead of them. He pushed and shoved along with the others towards it. And then up above him on a ledge of rock he saw a tall man with broad shoulders. It was his father! The cheering mounted as more men arrived. Suddenly a figure, smaller than his father stepped onto the ledge.

A space was cleared around him. Isaac squeezed his way through to the front. It was the stranger! He was sure it was, and something told him the stranger was indeed Mr Brunel! Here he was, the great man himself, standing next to his father, and cheering with him.

"Perfect! Not a bit out!" Mr Brunel said. Isaac followed his gaze to the roof of the tunnel and saw that the two parts of the tunnel met exactly.

"They said it couldn't be done, said it was impossible!" Mr Brunel thrust his hand in the air. Then he pulled a ring from his finger. He breathed on the ring, and rubbed it on his trousers.

As he held it up again Isaac saw the ring
twinkle in the candlelight. It was gold. And
then, unbelievably Mr Brunel was giving the
gleaming gold ring to his father! Isaac
pushed sideways through the knot of
workers, unable to stop himself.

"Father, Father," but his voice was drowned by Mr Brunel's.

"Go on take it man. You're a ganger I'm proud of – as I'm proud of you all. Now we will be able to travel down the railway line from London to Bristol and over the seas to New York." His father was fingering the ring, lost for words. Isaac rushed up to him.

"Father it's me."

"What the…?"

"Why the boy who draws trees! Your son I believe!"

"Yes, yes, my son, though how he got here..." Mr Brunel clamped a hand on Isaac's shoulder.

"Keep on with your drawing, boy. This all started with a drawing you know. By the way how *did* you get in here?"

"Down the shaft, Sir." Mr Brunel grinned and looked at Isaac's father.

"Adventurous lad you've got there. He'll go far." Isaac felt his father brush against him and knew he wasn't angry with him.

"There will be celebrating tonight, Isaac. Tell Gran I'll be very late. This is a special day."

"Special enough to go and see Mr Brunel's iron steamship, Father?" His father laughed.

"It certainly is.
Tell Gran we'll go on
Sunday for certain."

"And you be sure
to sketch my ship
young man," said
Mr Brunel smiling.

Glossary

bufflehead   a nineteenth-century word, meaning 'fool'

excavate   to excavate something is to dig it up

ganger   a foreman in charge of a gang of labourers

gin   a mechanism which was used for lowering large tubs down mine shafts

navvy   this word was first used in the nineteenth century to describe a labourer employed in the excavation and construction of earthworks such as canals, railways and tunnels

portal   a door, gate or gateway of elaborate design

shaft   a deep hole excavated down through a hill to a tunnel floor enabling men to go underground to work

stay   a post placed against the earth walls of a mine to strengthen them and give them firm support

tub   an open vessel, like a bucket, that carried navvies down tunnel shafts